Chapter 1

One minute Arjo was with me. The next minute he was missing.

We were on a school visit to the power station. We had come in two buses. We were in groups of ten. Each group had a grown-up. I was in Mrs Scott's group. Arjo was with Miss Teal.

A lady was talking about the generators. She said they were driven by super-heated steam.

Mr Saffrey was facing us. His eyes darted from face to face. Once the lady said something that was hard to follow. Mr Saffrey said it again in an easier way.

But where was Arjo? We had got out of the buses together. We had stayed together all the time. Now, I couldn't see him anywhere. How could he have gone missing?

I looked round the group again. I looked slowly this time. I looked at the backs of heads. I crept sideways so that I could look at a different angle. I had to make sure.

Arjo wasn't with us. This time I was certain.

The lady stopped talking. I went over to Miss Teal. 'Have you seen Arjo?' I asked. She looked concerned. 'No,' she said. 'Isn't he with you, Kat?'

What happened next made me feel very frightened. Suddenly bells rang. Lights flashed. Sirens wailed.

Something really scary was happening. This was an emergency, and Arjo was missing.

Chapter 2

A man ran up to Mr Saffrey. He spoke to him in a low, urgent voice. We could see something was wrong.

Mr Saffrey looked worried. 'Right everyone,' he said. 'I want you all to go back to the buses. Stay in your groups. Nobody run. And go quietly. I don't want any fuss.'

I felt myself panic. I knew this had something to do with Arjo. I broke away from the group and ran up to Mr Saffrey.

My mouth was dry. When I spoke, my voice sounded odd, as if I had wool in my mouth. It didn't sound like my voice. 'It's Arjo, isn't it?' I said. 'Where is he? What's happened to him?'

Mr Saffrey put his hand on my shoulder. 'Listen, Kat,' he said. 'Keep calm. A man has got Arjo. He's taken him hostage.'

I felt terrified. 'Where are they?' I asked.

'They're in the main control room,' said Mr Saffrey. 'I can't tell you a lot more. Try not to worry. The police are on their way.'

'But why?' I asked. 'Why would a man take Arjo hostage? Why here?'

Chapter 3

The lady in the white coat tried to smile. She bent down and put her arm round me. She was being kind, but I didn't want kindness. I didn't want to be treated like a child.

'We don't know much, yet,' she said. 'The man is making a protest. He says that the power station harms the environment. It causes acid rain. He wants us to shut it down.'

'But why has he got Arjo?' I asked. 'What has Arjo to do with it?'

Mr Saffrey spoke. 'He can't have planned that. He just came across us. He saw some children, so he took Arjo. He must think that having Arjo will help his protest.'

I saw people in orange jackets running. I heard more sirens. Some police cars raced up. I wondered how many more were on the way.

The lady spoke to Mr Saffrey. 'I think you'd better take Kat back to school,' she said.

I began to panic again.

'No!' I shouted. 'No! I'm not going. I've got to stay here. Tell the man to let Arjo go.'

The lady looked at me. 'I wish we could,' she said.

I tried to sound calm. 'Then let me be the hostage instead of Arjo,' I said, 'or let me go in with him.'

Chapter 4

Mr Saffrey understood. 'I know you would do that for Arjo,' he said. 'But you know we can't let you.'

Then he said, 'We must send for Kat and Arjo's parents but I think Kat ought to stay. I'll stay too.'

The wailing of sirens was getting louder. Two police trucks screamed to a stop. Twenty or thirty police officers piled out of the trucks.

Then I saw something that made
my blood run cold. The police were
wearing flak jackets to protect
themselves.

Flak jackets! Why? Was the man
with Arjo armed? I found myself
saying a prayer. 'Please let Arjo be all
right,' I said over and over. 'Please let
Arjo be all right.'

The next half-hour was terrible.
People seemed to be running
everywhere. I wanted the lights to
stop flashing and the sirens to stop
wailing.

Mr Saffrey held my hand tightly.
I'm glad he did.

Suddenly, the bells and sirens
stopped. Everything went quiet. The
silence was almost as bad as the
noise.

Then we heard a voice. It came from a loudspeaker.

'The area is now sealed off. The subject is in the main control room. He is holding a ten year old boy named Joseph Wilson.' It was odd to hear Arjo's real name – Joseph.

I held my breath. 'Don't let this be happening,' I said. 'Please!'

But the voice went on: 'The subject has explosives.'

Explosives! I felt as if my insides were filled with ice. My knees turned to jelly.

Chapter 5

Mr Saffrey put his hand on my arm. 'Listen, Kat, we must get hold of your parents,' he said. 'Do you know where they are?'

The thing was, I didn't know where my parents were. Maybe that sounds stupid, but Mum and Dad own a firm called Wilson Express. They deliver goods all over the country. They have two lorries and they both drive.

Dad is away a lot. He does the long runs. I knew he was in France.

Mum wasn't on the road all the time. But I knew she was away today. The trouble was I didn't know where. I was never very interested.

I told Mr Saffrey all this. Then Inspector Webb arrived. She asked me all over again. 'Kat,' she said, 'do you have any idea where they are? You say your dad's in France. How about your mum?'

All I knew was that Mum wouldn't be back until tomorrow. Tammy was going to look after us.

'We'll find your mum,' said Inspector Webb. ' We'll put out an alert on all motorways. We'll get her here as quickly as we can. Is there anyone we can contact now?'

There was nobody. My grand-parents lived miles away. So did Mum's sister, Auntie Viv.

'I see,' said Inspector Webb. 'Then I want you to be here to help Arjo. You'd better see this.'

They had set up a television screen. It showed the main control room.

I looked at the screen. It showed Arjo and the man who was holding him hostage.

Chapter 6

The man had his arm on Arjo's shoulder. You could tell he was holding Arjo tightly. Arjo's eyes were darting from left to right. He looked pretty scared.

I looked at the man. I was quite surprised. I imagined he would look different. I expected him to look young. I thought he might wear jeans, and have long hair and a beard. I was wrong.

The man looked quite old. He didn't look like a terrorist. He looked quite smart. I guessed that was how he got into the power station in the first place.

He had grey hair and he wore glasses. He was wearing a shirt and tie. He looked as if he worked in a bank or an office.

I wanted to shout at him. I wanted to yell, 'Let Arjo go. Arjo isn't part of your plan. Arjo hasn't done you any harm.'

The man was talking on a mobile telephone. He moved as he spoke, pushing Arjo in front of him.

The man turned and I saw his back. That was when I saw them: four little packages strapped to his waist. They were connected to a battery. The packages had wires coming from them.

I knew what they were – explosives! And there was Arjo – next to a madman with explosives strapped to his body.

Chapter 7

I felt myself panic again. Inspector Webb spoke to me. Her voice was very calm.

'Listen, Kat. The man won't do anything dangerous. He's making a protest. He wants everyone to hear a message. He's got what he wants – time.'

I looked blank. 'What do you mean – time?' I asked.

'The longer he stays there, the more people hear about his protest. He wants to make demands. He wants the world to hear his story. Now he's got Arjo. It's a big story.'

I looked for Mr Saffrey, but he'd gone. Why had he left me? I felt alone and confused. Why did he go without saying a word?

Then Mr Saffrey was back. I heard him arguing with someone. I heard him say: 'Najma is Kat's friend. I think she should be with her. She can support Kat until Kat's mum gets here.'

I don't know how Mr Saffrey had done it. He had Najma with him. I wanted to hug him. Najma ran over to me. It was so good to have her with me. I felt a little better.

As it happened, Najma turned out to be pretty useful.

Chapter 8

Inspector Webb began to talk to me. 'Tell us about Arjo,' she said.

'There's not much to tell,' I said. 'His hearing is impaired. He has to wear two hearing aids. They help him hear most sounds. He's learned to watch people's lips. He lip-reads what people are saying to him.'

'He's very bright,' put in Mr
Saffrey, 'and he's very observant.
He's good with his hands. He
mended the school tape recorder.'

'I see,' said the policewoman. 'So
will he understand what's happening
to him?'

I felt angry. 'Of course he will,' I
said, crossly.

Mr Saffrey looked cross, too. 'Arjo is highly intelligent. His problem is he can't hear, not that he doesn't understand.'

Then Najma spotted something. 'What is Arjo doing?' she said. 'His face looks odd.'

30

We all stared at the television
screen. Arjo's mouth was moving. He
looked as if he was chewing slowly.
He was moving his hands, too. They
made strange, slow movements.

'I can't think what he's doing,' I
said. 'Can we get a closer view of
him?'

We all stared at the screen, 'Sorry,' said Inspector Webb. 'We can't. It's only a security camera. But Arjo has seen it. He's looking straight at it.'

It was true! Arjo had spotted where the camera was. He was making faces at it. I wondered why. Then I realized what Arjo was doing.

Chapter 9

Arjo was communicating with us. He was talking silently and making signs – but in slow motion. He was doing it so that the man wouldn't notice.

Arjo has always had to lip-read. He doesn't use sign language. But he does use his hands to help him say things. I know how he communicates. I should do – he's my brother.

I could see that Arjo was trying to say something. The trouble was, I couldn't tell what it was.

Then Najma had an idea. 'All this is on video. Play the video on fast forward. It will speed up Arjo's movements. Then we will see what he's trying to say.'

It took a little while to set this up. Arjo went on moving his lips and making the signs. He was saying the same thing over and over.

At last the video was ready to play back. We all stared at it. Then it ran fast forward and I could make out what Arjo was saying.

He was saying that the man was harmless. The explosives were a fake. The wires weren't connected to anything.

He asked why no one was talking to him. He pointed to his receiver.

It's funny how you miss obvious things! Why hadn't I thought of it sooner? He was wearing his receiver. He had worn it on the outing. He had it to hear the talk about the power station.

Of course! We could speak to Arjo.

Chapter 10

I told Inspector Webb what Arjo was saying. 'If Arjo is right, he's not in so much danger,' I said. 'We could tell him to run for it. Then you could rush in and overpower the man.'

Inspector Webb shook her head. 'We can't risk it,' she said. 'How does Arjo know the explosives are fake? He can't know for sure. What if he's wrong?'

I could see Inspector Webb's point. All the same, I knew Arjo wasn't wrong.

Someone handed me the little microphone and transmitter. Now I could talk to Arjo. I spoke quietly at first. 'Arjo! Arjo!' I whispered. 'It's me, Kat. Nod if you can hear me.'

I saw at once that Arjo had heard my voice. He nodded at the camera and gave a little smile.

'We got your signals,' I said. 'Are you sure the explosives aren't real?'

Arjo nodded slowly.

I had to tell Arjo not to risk anything. 'Don't try and run,' I said. 'Just wait. We'll get you out. Mum and Dad will be here soon.'

Arjo couldn't speak back. He had to signal again. He made the same slow movements. It took a long time. At last we played them back on the video recorder.

This time Arjo said he was thirsty. He wanted some water. Lots of water. In fact he wanted three big bottles of fizzy water.

'Three big bottles?' said the Inspector.

'He has to drink a lot – all the time,' I fibbed. 'He likes fizzy water. He drinks it all the time.'

I knew he was up to something. Of course, I didn't know what.

Chapter 11

The police couldn't find Mum.
They'd found her lorry near Leeds.
It was parked in a service station. It
was locked, and Mum wasn't with it.

Then I remembered. Mum had a
friend near Leeds. If Mum had time,
she'd stop. Her friend would drive
out and fetch her. I guessed that
Mum was with her friend now.

'Can you remember where your mum's friend lives?' asked Inspector Webb. I shook my head. I had no idea.

'Try and think what the friend's name is,' said the Inspector.

I felt stupid, but I didn't even know her full name. Well, I knew she was called Alison, but that was all.

'We'll keep trying to find her,' said Inspector Webb, 'so don't worry.'

It was odd to think of Mum in Leeds. She would be enjoying a good chat with Alison - not knowing what was going on. Not knowing Arjo was a hostage in a power station.

Najma squeezed my hand. I longed for Mum to be here. Without her, I had to keep strong for Arjo's sake.

Chapter 12

The man had a list of demands. Inspector Webb was right. What he wanted most was publicity.

The man wanted all power stations to close down for a day. He wanted people to think about how they live. He said that we rely too much on electricity. Power stations harm the environment.

He was talking on his mobile phone. We could see him on the television screen. He seemed to be getting very restless. He moved about a lot.

'Why is he so twitchy?' asked Inspector Webb.

Then we realized what was upsetting the man. The tray of food must have arrived. We could see Arjo telling the man he wanted a drink.

The man looked at Arjo. Then he quickly went to the door and opened it slowly. A tray was on the floor outside. On it was some food and the three large bottles of fizzy water Arjo had asked for.

The man picked up the tray. He carried it across to Arjo and put it on a table.

I thought that Arjo wanted to drink the water. Then he'd have to go to the loo. Maybe that was how Arjo could get away.

Arjo had other ideas.

Chapter 13

Arjo unscrewed the top of one bottle. We watched him slowly loosen the tops of the others.

I spoke into the microphone. 'Arjo,' I said, urgently. 'Don't do anything stupid.'

Arjo looked at the camera. I saw him wink slightly. 'Oh no,' I thought. 'He is up to something.'

Then Arjo moved with lightning
speed. Suddenly he threw one of the
bottles down – then another. He
threw them as hard as he could. They
smacked on the floor right behind the
man.

Have you ever seen a bottle of fizzy water hit the floor really hard? It's like a water bomb.

Both bottles split open. The water sprayed out. One bottle actually shot back up in the air. Two fountains of water sprayed over Arjo and the man.

At the same time Arjo shook the other bottle. A jet of water shot out. It hit the man full in the back.

The man was taken by surprise. He crouched into a ball to stop himself being soaked.

Then Arjo ran for the door.

Chapter 14

By the time Mum got to us, it was all over. The man had been arrested and taken away.

As for Arjo, I didn't know if he'd done the right thing or not.

I could hardly believe it when I knew that Arjo was safe. I found myself shaking all over. I couldn't stop myself.

When I saw Arjo I was still shaking. I gave him a hug, but he pushed me away. He looked at me and grinned. 'Why are you shaking?' he asked. 'It was me who was taken hostage.'

Was I pleased to see Mum! They had flown her down from Leeds in a helicopter. It must have taken her some courage. I know how much she hates flying.

Mum was glad it was all over. 'I just can't believe all this has happened,' she said. Mum said she felt angry with the man. 'What right did he have to hold Arjo like that?' she said. 'Think what he's put us all through.'

Inspector Webb looked serious. 'That was a very dangerous thing to do, Arjo,' she said. 'You couldn't be sure the man had fake explosives.'

Arjo gave one of his big grins. 'I could see they were fake,' he said. 'Anybody could.'

It was true. The fizzy water had hit the man's back. It had soaked the little packets on the man's belt. The packets fell apart. Bits of paper hung down in soggy strips.

I thought of the man. He had given us all a terrible time. Maybe his protest was a good one. I don't know. Had he got the right to do what he did?

Mr Saffrey looked relieved. 'It's been quite a day,' he said. He looked at Arjo, Najma, and me. 'If you like, you can have the day off tomorrow.'

54

Arjo grinned again. 'And miss telling everyone about my water bomb idea? I'd rather come to school.'

Level 1

The Hole in the Ground
Hidden Gold
The Flying Armchair
I Hate Computers!
The Night it Rained Chips
Toxic Waste

More Level 1

People Like That
Andy the Hero
Fair Scare
It Can't Be
Blaze!
A Good Tip

Level 2

Funny Sort of Treasure
Arjo's Bike
In the Net
Million-Dollar Egg
The Exploding Parrot
The Pool Party

Level 3

Siren Green
Remote Control
Blazing Burgers
Skydive Wedding
Electric Sandwiches
The Copper Cockerel

Level 4

Who's Kooza?
Ghost
In the End
Let's Hear It for Nan
Hostage!
Dirt Bike Rider

Level 5

Black Holme Island
Who Kidnapped the Mayor?
Scottish Adventure
Alien
Sleepover Shock
Last Term at Wolf Hill